Thank you, Mom, Dad, Brian, and Colin — C.R.

tiger tales
5 River Road, Suite 128, Wilton, CT 06897
Published in the United States 2016
First published in Great Britain 2006 by Little Tiger Press
Text and illustrations copyright © 2006 Catherine Rayner
ISBN-13: 978-1-68010-005-1
ISBN-10: 1-68010-005-X
Printed in China
LTP/1800/1245/0915
10 9 8 7 6 5 4 3 2 1

For more insight and activities, visit us at
www.tigertalesbooks.com

AUGUSTUS AND HIS SMILE

by CATHERINE RAYNER

tiger tales

Augustus the tiger was sad.
He had lost his smile.

So he did a HUGE tigery stretch

and set off to find it.

First he crept
under a cluster
of bushes. He found
a small, shiny beetle,
but he couldn't see
his smile.

Then he climbed to the tops of the tallest trees.
He found birds that chirped and called,
but he couldn't find his smile.

Further and further Augustus searched.

He scaled the crests of the highest mountains where the snow clouds swirled, making   frost patterns in the   freezing air.

He swam to the bottom of the deepest ocean
and splished and splashed with shoals of tiny, shiny fish.

He pranced and paraded through the
largest desert, making shadow shapes
in the sun. Augustus padded further

and further

through shifting sand

until . . .

. . . pitter-
    patter,
        pitter-
            patter,

            drip,

                drop,

                    plop!

Augustus danced and raced as raindrops bounced and flew.

He splashed
through puddles,

bigger and deeper.

He raced toward
a huge,
silver-blue puddle and saw . . .

. . . there, under his nose

. . . his smile!

And Augustus realized that his smile would be there
whenever he was happy.

He only had to swim with the fish
or dance in the puddles
or climb the mountains and look at the world—
for happiness was everywhere around him.

Augustus was so happy that
he hopped

and skipped . . .

. . . and jumped away,
smiling.